MANY WINTERS

Prose and Poetry of the Pueblos

by Nancy Wood

Drawings and Paintings

by

Frank Howell

MANY WINTERS

Doubleday & Company, Inc.

GARDEN CITY, NEW YORK

Library of Congress Cataloging in Publication Data

Wood, Nancy C
Many winters.
1. Taos Indians—Poetry.   2. Taos Indians.
I. Howell, Frank, illus.   II. Title.
PS3573.0595M3   811'.5'4
ISBN 0-385-02226-3 Trade
0-385-02238-7 Pre-Bound
Library of Congress Catalog Card Number 74–3554

9 8 7 6 5 4

INTRODUCTION

You know how it is.
People come here and they want to know our secret of life.
They ask many questions but their minds are already made up.
They admire our children but they feel sorry for them.
They look around and they do not see anything except dust.
They come to our dances but they are always wanting to take
pictures.
They come into our homes expecting to learn about us in five
minutes.
Our homes, which are made of mud and straw, look strange to them.
They are glad they do not live here.
Yet they are not sure whether or not we know something which is
the key to all understanding.
Our secret of life would take them forever to find out.
Even then, they would not believe it.

The words came from an old Indian at Taos Pueblo who sat on the
roof of his house one afternoon, his back to the sun. He sat wrapped
in his cotton blanket, his long hair in two braids. His face was wrin-
kled and the color of the earth from which his adobe house was
made.

To the east, Taos Mountain rose sharply behind the pueblo. Near the top of it was Blue Lake, a lake where the spirits of the Indians go when they die. Blue Lake is sacred to the Taos and it is the source of all life to them.

To the west, in the rosy light of late afternoon, was the Rio Grande Valley, stretching on for a hundred miles or more. It had once belonged to the Taos, long before the Spaniards came in 1598. For the next three hundred years, the Taos lands were gradually taken away, first by Spain, then by Mexico, and finally by the United States Government which took the most of all. What land the Taos have left today is still more than any of the eighteen other tribes along the Rio Grande. It is also the richest and most beautiful and therefore the most coveted by the white man.

The old Indian talked of many things that day. The seasons coming and going. His corn growing tall in the field. His youth and his memories of his elders. He spoke of the white man, too. He neither trusted nor respected him. He was concerned about the white man's intrusion into his everyday life.

Over the years that I had known him, the old Indian had told me many things about this simple and meaningful life. With him, and with others of the tribe whose friendship I had enjoyed for many years, I began to learn what is perhaps "the key to all understanding." It has been so at least for me.

The name of this old Indian is not important. Nor are the names of any of the people I have known at Taos Pueblo for a long time. What is important is the fact that this tribe, which has been there in New Mexico for eight hundred years or more, is still in existence. Their religion and their way of life are intact because they have not let the scientists or the do-gooders in. They prefer to be left alone. Yet the threat to them grows daily. The government, which recently failed to take Blue Lake away from the Taos, threatens now to take their water supply which runs down through the pueblo from Blue Lake. Civilization presses dangerously near with new roads, increasing populations, and ski resorts. Can the Taos survive? One of their beliefs is that the white man will eventually destroy himself. He has no roots, they say. Without this, a man or a tribe cannot survive. When the white civilization falls, the Taos will remain. They are as positive of this as they are that the sun will rise in the morning. How can they be so sure?

The white man would call it blind faith. The Taos call it a way of life. They believe it is stronger than governments or gain. The old men speak of this philosophy in quiet voices that have much to say. I have tried to write down what they have passed on to me, not always in words, but in the expression of a life that is richly and fully lived.

Nancy Wood

Many winters I have lived
Ever since the beginning of time
When the first snow fell
Covering the tired earth
Which played with endless summer.
Many winters I held the water captive
On the tops of many mountains
Still warm from the earth's beginning
When the moon and the sun gave birth
To one full circle of beauty.
Many winters I blew the stars around
So that the place where each star fell
Was where a river grew
Taking as its course to the sea
The path of the winter sun.
Many winters the trees slept with me
And the animals walked on my breast
Just as the birds drew near
Seeking warmth from my fire
Which took the sting from the night.
Many winters I have been
Companion to the lonely moon
Chasing after the raging sun
Which listened to our song of thanks
Before releasing earth from winter.
Many winters I have lived
Ever since the beginning of time
When out of the melting snow
Came the first frail flower which said
I am the spirit of spring.

The tree in winter is like
The lines upon my father's face
Or like the paths I tried to take
When I was young searching
For one clear way to understanding.
In every branch I found
A smaller branch leading me
Toward many ends and many sorrows.
Too fragile to bear my weight,
All my branches broke
And I fell to the earth confused.
I saw the tree in winter
Reaching toward the sky
With bare branches tangled
Like so many paths and yet
Each path had a purpose,
Leading back to the roots of the tree.

You shall ask
What good are dead leaves
And I will tell you
They nourish the sore earth.
You shall ask
What reason is there for winter
And I will tell you
To bring about new leaves.
You shall ask
Why are the leaves so green
And I will tell you
Because they are rich with life.
You shall ask
Why must summer end
And I will tell you
So that the leaves can die.

Old Man Winter blew in on a cloud from the north
And lay down on the mountaintops
Covering them with snow.
His fingers reached down to the valleys below
Stealing the leaves from the trees.
His hands closed around the water
Gripping it with ice.
His breath roared out from his lips
Stopping all streams at their source.
The feet of Old Man Winter walked upon the earth
Freezing all the grass.
When he was through
Old Man Winter curled up and went to sleep
Drawing into himself
All beasts
All land
All men.

The earth is all that lasts.
The earth is what I speak to when
I do not understand my life
Nor why I am not heard.
The earth answers me with the same song
That it sang for my fathers when
Their tears covered up the sun.
The earth sings a song of gladness.
The earth sings a song of praise.
The earth rises up and laughs at me
Each time that I forget
How spring begins with winter
And death begins with birth.

When I look at ugliness, I see beauty.
When I am far from home, I see my old friends.
When there is noise, I hear a robin's song instead.
When I am in a crowd, it is the mountain's peace I feel.
In the winter of my sorrow, I remember the summer of my joy.
In the nighttime of my loneliness, I breathe the day of my
thanksgiving.
But when sadness spreads its blanket and that is what I see,
I take my eyes to some high place until I find
A reflection of what lies deep inside of me.

Now this is what we believe.
The mother of us all is earth.
The Father is the sun.
The Grandfather is the Creator
Who bathed us with his mind
And gave life to all things.
The Brother is the beasts and trees.
The Sister is that with wings.
We are the Children of Earth
And do it no harm in any way.
Nor do we offend the sun
By not greeting it at dawn.
We praise our Grandfather for his creation.
We share the same breath together—
The beasts, the trees, the birds, the man.

The land here is peaceful.
It is bathed in golden light which smoothes out
The edges of harshness so that everything is right.
With the sun always in our eyes we have a lazy vision which
Finds fault only on cloudy days.
Even in winter the land is soothing.
It rises and falls so gently that
Our eyes grow heavy following it to the horizon.
Here and there the sleeping trees reach out to the sky.
Here and there are our fields and horses, sleeping, sleeping.
Is it any wonder that we love the land the way we do?
We dance to the beat of it and perceive its rhythm as our own.

When the hand of winter gives up its grip to the sun
And the river's hard ice becomes the tongue to spring
I must go into the earth itself
To know the source from which I came.
Where there is a history of leaves
I lie face down upon the land.
I smell the rich wet earth
Trembling to allow the birth
Of what is innocent and green.
My fingers touch the yielding earth
Knowing that it contains
All previous births and deaths.
I listen to a cry of whispers
Concerning the awakening earth
In possession of itself.
With a branch between my teeth
I feel the growth of trees
Flowing with life born of ancient death.
I cover myself with earth
So that I may know while still alive
How sweet is the season of my time.

The skin of the earth
covers its imperfections
Just as my face conceals
my vast uncertainty.
In the dry cracks of the earth
I find that it has bled
Just as my spirit has bled
from the injuries of man.
The earth has healed itself
through time moving across
its tortured face of skin.
But what shall heal me except
the sun which makes cracks in my face
so that I can come together with my land.

With these hands I have held
a bird with a broken wing.
With these hands I have touched
my children in the sun.
With these hands I have made
a house of living earth.
With these hands I have worked
a field of growing corn.
With these hands I have learned to kill
As much as I have learned to live.
These hands are the tools of my spirit.
These hands are the warriors of my anger.
These hands are the limitations of my self.
These hands grow old and feel
unfamiliar walls
As they reach out to find
the world I used to know.

Reaching back from here
All that I remember of my life
Are the great round rocks and not
The unimportant stones.
I know that I experienced pain and yet
The scars have healed so that
I am like the tree covering itself
With new growth every year.
I know that I walked in sadness and yet
All that I remember now
Is the soothing autumn light.
I know that there was much to make my life unhappy
If I had stopped to notice how
The world sings a broken song.
But I preferred to dwell within
A universe of fields and streams
Which echoed the wholeness of my song.

When daylight shuts her eyes
And the sky is fast asleep,
The moon comes up with half a face
And the stars put holes in the night.

I am growing older knowing
That my disappearing youth
Hides itself in my uncertain wisdom
Growing younger all the time.

You are my children of laughter.
For you the moon will change its face.
For you the rainbow will rise full circle.
You are my children of hope.
For you the path will bend its destination.
For you the earth will forsake dry seasons.
You are my children of freedom.
For you the eagle will share its wings.
For you the wind will travel day and night.
You are my children of beauty.
For you the bird will give up its song.
For you the snow will fall with flowers.

All of my life is a dance.
When I was young and feeling the earth
My steps were quick and easy.
The beat of the earth was so loud
That my drum was silent beside it.
All of my life rolled out from my feet
Like my land which had no end as far as I could see.
The rhythm of my life was pure and free.
As I grew older my feet kept dancing so hard
That I wore a spot in the earth
At the same time I made a hole in the sky.
I danced to the sun and the rain
And the moon lifted me up
So that I could dance to the stars.
My head touched the clouds sometimes
And my feet danced deep in the earth
So that I became the music I danced to everywhere.
It was the music of life.
Now my steps are slow and hard
And my body fails my spirit.
Yet my dance is still within me and
My song is the air I breathe.
My song insists that I keep dancing forever.
My song insists that I keep rhythm
With all of the earth and the sky.
My song insists that I will never die.

Today is a very good day to die.
Every living thing is in harmony with me.
Every voice sings a chorus within me.
All beauty has come to rest in my eyes.
All bad thoughts have departed from me.
Today is a very good day to die.
My land is peaceful around me.
My fields have been turned for the last time.
My house is filled with laughter.
My children have come home.
Yes, today is a very good day to die.

My child, tomorrow's dawn will come up black
If there is rain behind your eyes.
The sun will bear the sky's dark fruit
If there is a shadow on your smile.
The smoke will never follow you
If your back is wet with fear.
The trees will not answer you
If your song is one of complaining.
You can see the dreams we had broken like our arrows
Or you can see the paths we took covered with many sorrows.
But if the earth lives inside of you
And you nourish her roots with your blood
Then you will grow as tall as the trees
And the moon will smile at your courage.

If I had known before
All the things I know today
I would have begun my life
As an old man tricked
By old men telling me
There was nothing to fear except
Leaving my youth behind.
What would have been the fun of that?
What home would my mistakes have had?
It is better this way.
Now I can wish
For my youth to come back
Just so I can tell it how
Old age is nothing but remembering
How rich the green fields looked
Despite the lack of rain.

In the distance of my years I cover myself with time
Like a blanket which enfolds me with the layers of my life.
What can I tell you except that I have gone
nowhere and everywhere?
What can I tell you except that I have not begun
my journey now that it is through?
All that I ever was and am yet to be
lies within me now this way.

There is the Young Boy in me traveling east
With the Eagle which taught me to see far and wide.
The Eagle took his distance and said,
There is a Time for Rising Above
So that you do not think
Your small world too important.
There is a time for turning your vision toward the sky.

There is the Young Girl in me traveling west
With the Bear which taught me to look inside.
The Bear stood by himself and said,
There is a Time for Being Alone
So that you do not take on
The appearance of your friends.
There is a time for being at home with yourself.

There is the Old Man in me traveling north
With the Buffalo which taught me wisdom.
The Buffalo disappeared and said,

There is a Time for Believing Nothing
So that you do not speak
What you have already heard.
There is a Time for Keeping Quiet.

There is the Old Woman in me traveling south
With the Mouse which taught me my limitations.
The Mouse lay close to the ground and said,
There is a Time for Taking Comfort in Small Things
So that you do not feel
Forgotten in the night.
There is a Time for enjoying the Worm.

> That is the way it was.
> That is the way it shall continue
> With the Eagle and the Bear
> With the Buffalo and the Mouse
> In all directions joined with me
> To form the circle of my life.

I am an Eagle.
The small world laughs at my deeds.
But the great sky keeps to itself
My thoughts of immortality.

I am a Bear.
In my solitude I resemble the wind.
I blow the clouds together
So they form images of my friends.

I am a Buffalo.
My voice echoes inside my mouth.
All that I have learned of life
I share with the smoke of my fire.

I am a Mouse.
My life is beneath my nose.
Each time that I journey toward the horizon
I find a hole instead.

The hands that I remember
were of my father cutting down the tree
Asking forgiveness for its death.
The hands that I remember
were of my mother showing me
The purpose of a flower.
The hands that I remember
were of my brother killing rabbits
So he might later kill the deer.
The hands that I remember
were of my sister digging earth
To discover a newborn tree.
The hands that I remember
were of my grandfather teaching me
The way to the mountain of my life.

Remember when our land smelled sweet? Remember when our corn
was good? Remember when everything was rich and beautiful?

No. I do not remember that.

I think that television has ruined our imaginations.
I used to look at clouds and see eagles and lions.
Now I look at them and see automobiles.

My dog barks because he cannot speak.
My horse whinnys because he cannot laugh.
My sheep bleats because he cannot cry.
My rooster crows because he cannot boast.
But my cat just goes to sleep because
He is too old to complain.

Every winter my father rode his pony out to the buffalo. In those days they roamed freely. It was the Time of Taking Away however, and the buffalo did not last long.

After he killed a buffalo, my father would eat the warm liver raw. He liked the taste of it. Then my father would warm his hands inside the buffalo. After that he would skin the buffalo and cut up the meat. Nothing went to waste. He brought the meat home and hung it on that hook which is still in the ceiling.

We had plenty of meat all winter long. It did not cost anything. And we did not need a license either.

To be yourself is to be
Alone with the wind crying
When all that you ask for is
The warmth of a human fire.

We are not important.
Our lives are simply threads
Pulling along the lasting thoughts
Which travel through time that way.

We have always had a religion. We have always believed in God and worshiped Him in our own way. It was not until the Spaniards came (in 1598) that we were told that God is a human being who lives up above the clouds somewhere. We were also told that there was a son of this god who came to live on the earth. He died in a horrible way to save us and that is why we were supposed to worship him.

At that time, these ideas were strange. To us, God was in rocks and trees and sky everywhere. We had the sun as our father and the earth as our mother; the moon and the stars were our brothers. We had never seen God as a human being before until the Spaniards came. Then the friars in their long brown robes went around with crossed sticks and prayers and water which they poured on our heads. They told us that we belonged to their religion because they had just baptized us into it. Some of us mistook these friars for gods. Some of us resisted their religion because we were afraid of it. Some of us were beaten or put to death.

In the end we decided it did not make much difference what church there was on the outside. We have always had a church within ourselves. This is the one which counts. This is the one which will remain long after all of the outside churches have fallen down.

The rock strengthens me.
The river rushing through me
Cleanses
Insists
That I keep moving toward
A distant light
A quiet place
Where I can be
Continuous
And in rhythm with
The song of summer
That you have given me.

What can I do when I feel the world's harsh breath and know
That if I stay too long in its path
My path shall be burned up also.
I must go back to the land again
And find the eagle at home with the rock.
I must climb to the mountaintop
And find the spot where the river begins.
I must lie quietly beside the earth
And find the warmth of its heart.
I must turn my vision to the sky
And find the purpose of clouds.
Then trouble seems far away
And the breath which consumes all beauty
Has passed right over me.

I wandered as half a river
My waters going nowhere.
I wandered without a shadow
My body alone in the sun.
I wandered as a rootless tree
The earth not knowing me.
I wandered as a wingless bird
The sky forgetting me.
I was lightning with no thunder.
I was a flower with no rain.
I was a stranger to spring
And winter was home to me.
At last my summer came.
She was the moon to my setting sun.
She was the rain to my hungry earth.
She was spring to my melting snow.
Wherever she went there went my thunder also.

Now I will tell you a story about dying. It is a beautiful story and should not make you sad.

When autumn was coming, I went along the path to the mountain. The sun was shining brightly and gave to the leaves a gorgeous color. The stream danced slowly over the rocks and made a Song of Departure. The birds too were telling me that the season was coming to an end.

But there was no sadness anywhere because all was as it should be and had been and would be forever. You see, nature does not fight against anything. When it comes time to die, there is rejoicing. The new circle of life begins with the death of the old one and so there is a celebration on every level.

As I went along the path, I saw that there was much preparation and much in the way of the Last Dance also.

On the trunk of a golden aspen tree, there were two butterflies who had come to die. Their wings folded and unfolded slowly. It was hard for them to breathe. As the sun warmed them, the butterflies began to dance with one another. It was their Last Dance. The slow music of the stream and the gentle voice of the wind gave them something beautiful to die to. The butterflies were not afraid either. They danced until the sun fell into the earth for the night. Then they fell into the earth and nourished it.

When spring came again, I noticed that on the trunk of the fresh green aspen tree there were two new butterflies. They were dancing with one another. It was a Mating Dance. The stream was swift and pure and new again. The song it made for the butterflies was a Song of Beginning Life.

I have lived surrounded by the earth on six sides.
It is all around me.
It is above my head and beneath my feet.
It is in four directions also.
My house is made of the Earth Itself.
My house is a mother to me.
When I die, my house will come with me.
When I die, My house will surround me on six sides.
My house made of the Earth Itself
Is a house of Death's Companion also.

You say to me,
Old Man who dwells in last year,
Old Man who sings old songs,
Wake up and see
The world as it really is.
I say to you,
Young Man who lives nowhere,
Young Man who hears only noise,
The world has grown within me
And I am rich with years.

Who will teach me now that my fathers
Have gone with the buffalo?
Who will tell of times I wish I knew?
Who will direct my journey
So that I will come out right?
The years are clouds which
Cover my ancestors.
Let them sleep.
I shall find my way alone.

When I was young I did not know anything.
Although I was very tall, I had never grown.
So one day I went to the mountain
To die a little death.
This is the way of my people
In order to become purified.
My mouth opened and my cry fell
On the wind which blew it away.
My eyes saw nothing and so
The sun blinded my ignorance.
My ears heard only silence and so
The river drowned me in song.
My hands stopped the air and so
The fire fed upon me.
At last I was reduced to nothing.
Then one day I woke up.
Speak the truth said the wind
And I said I am afraid.
See the reason said the sun
And I saw my village changing.
Listen to the music said the river
And I heard my people laughing.
Feel the warmth said the fire
And I held my children in my arms.
Know what you are said the spirit
And I said I am a man.

What can I tell you of life?
It comes hard-earned and beautiful.
It comes disguised and tricked.
It comes with laughter too.
What can I tell you of life?
Nothing.
My version of it is my own.
It does not belong to you.
Like trees, we have our common roots.
But our growth is very different.

My people are a multitude of one.
Many voices are within them.
Many lives they have lived as various Beings.
They could have been a bear, a lion, an eagle or even
A rock, a river or a tree.
Who knows?
All of these Beings are within them.
They can use them any time they want.
On some days it is good to be a tree
Looking out in all directions at once.
On some days it is better to be a rock
Saying nothing and blind to everything.
On some days the only thing to do is
To fight fiercely like a lion.
Then, too, there are reasons for being an eagle.
When life becomes too hard here
My people can fly away and see
How small the earth really is.
Then they can laugh and come back home again.

You cannot go back.
You cannot live here believing that
Our way is the bridge to yesterday.
Now is not the way it was.
Now is beautiful because
Everything that mattered
Has found its way to us.

There are no dark times.
There are only people with
sawdust in their eyes.
No wonder they look at
the great rolling land and see
only doors and windows.
No wonder they look at
the tall mountains and see
only a way to make them tame.
No wonder they look at
the endless sky and see
only a journey to the moon.
There are no dark times.
There are only moments which
are discolored like
sand which is wet with rain.
There are only moments which
give pain like
the sting of a bumblebee.
There are only moments which
are as cruel as
the death of an eagle by a gun.
There are no dark times.
I know this because
Tomorrow receives the best in time
Or else it would not come.

Do you know what is wrong with the white people?
They have no roots.
They are always trying to plant themselves and yet
They will blow away in the wind because
They are born with wheels.

Brother, you fight against me.
Brother, you do not see that we cannot live
Except as what we are.
Brother, you have listened to a different song.
You have danced a different dance.
Brother, how can I hold you to me now
When I do not know your face?

I have found more to life
In the travels of an ant
Than in the progress of the world
Which has fallen far behind
The place it started from.

What the white man does to us follows a pattern.

First they come to us offering presents which we do not need. Then they offer to buy our land which is not ours to sell. The land does not belong to anyone. It was put here to be thanked and used gently. The land belongs to itself, just like the moon and the stars.

But to the white man such an idea is crazy. To him, everything has to be used up. Then it is worth something. That is why they will do anything to take our homes and destroy us. All of our brothers to the east had this happen and many of our brothers to the west also. What can we do? If we fight, they will not educate our children to their way which is all we are left with now. If we do not fight, they will help themselves to our life.

This time the white man wants our water which flows out of our sacred Blue Lake. It flows through our land and down into the pueblo where we use it for drinking and cooking and washing. It nourishes our crops as well. It is all we have. The white man does not need it. It is so small anyway, just enough for us and for our children. We have been careful with the water which flows from Blue Lake and it will last forever.

When the white man gave Blue Lake back to us, some of us said, it will not end here. The white man is angry because he has had to give up this land which was ours to begin with, ever since we were put here as a people by the Great Father. We said, the white man will think of some new way to get what he wants. And now that has happened.

If the white man takes our water, what do we have left? The land is no good without it. And we will shrivel up and die.

What we have to do now is walk quietly among them. They have every weapon there is. We have only what we believe. Perhaps they will listen to us. Perhaps they will not. But we are a people of strong beliefs. Our hearts are where they should be. Everything is in place here. We are going on together. They cannot kill us.

I know what you think. That we will be swallowed up. What are we that we can possibly hold out against the world? It has been coming at us a long time, coaxing us to put on white faces so that we will all look alike. We cannot understand this obsession to change us, to put our land to what is called use, nor to make us think thoughts which are not our own.

Why can't we be left alone? There are so few of us and our lands are not vast nor do we possess anything of value to them. Every time a tribe has been swallowed up it is because they have stood in the way of a great devouring tide which began in the east and is not through yet.

The white man will not get down on his knees to look at the earth. He views it from up above. He does not see the importance of ants. He does not see the beauty of a spider's thread. He is never there to watch the earth turning over. He does not care to know how the cricket sounds.

How can we be any different? How can we go around pretending that money and possessions will make us happy? All the time the white man tells us we need more things. To pay for them, we would have to sell our spirit. They do not tell us that, but we know it to be true because it has happened to many tribes. Where are they now? Trying to be Indians again. But you know they cannot go back. They are without land. They are without roots. That is why we fight so hard.

I remember you when
The tame rose sleeps
Between the jaws of winter.
I remember you when
The humming insects mother
The newborn leaves of spring.
I remember you when
The argument of frogs becomes
The laughing song of summer.
I remember you when
I hear my corn begin to grow
And beauty crowds my life.

Here I am in the winter of my years
Having lived with you since spring and yet
Where did autumn go?

A long time I have lived with you
And now we must be going
Separately to be together.
Perhaps I shall be the wind
To blur your smooth waters
So that you do not see your face too much.
Perhaps I shall be the star
To guide your uncertain wings
So that you have direction in the night.
Perhaps I shall be the fire
To separate your thoughts
So that you do not give up.
Perhaps I shall be the rain
To open up the earth
So that your seed may fall.
Perhaps I shall be the snow
To let your blossoms sleep
So that you may bloom in spring.
Perhaps I shall be the stream
To play a song on the rock
So that you are not alone.
Perhaps I shall be a new mountain
So that you always have a home.

I am a woman.
I hold up half of the sky.
I am a woman.
I nourish half of the earth.
I am a woman.
The rainbow touches my shoulders.
The universe encircles my eyes.

Woman of the mountains
Lying face up to the sky
What do you know of old stars born
When you were young
With raindrops forming tears
For all the stars which died.
What has the moon told you of loneliness
With its sad face fixed on yours
Waiting forever to be touched
By the mothering sun.
What song does the wind play for you
As it lingers on your breast
And hollows out the softness of your thighs.
Who has kept you company through the ages
As the earth turned green beneath you
And the river flowed from your eyes.
Woman of the mountains
Lying face up to the sun
When will you know
The generosity of time
To crumble your unmoving body
Into mine.

Wherever my eyes fall
I see you everywhere.
In the still pond gathering ice
To conceal itself from winter
You are the deep shy water.
In the slow built sparrow's nest
Of infinite eggs and seasons
You are the mother to spring.
In summer flowers bursting
Down from the mountaintop
You are a wild and fragile dancer.
In the autumn wind at odds
With the disappearing leaves
You are the promise of next year.
Wherever my eyes fall
I see you everywhere.
You have thus become my vision
As my eyes go blind with years.

Old Woman,
It is you.
It was you even when
I did not see you except
In the eyes of my spirit.
Old Woman,
With you I saw
The dead log giving life
And the mid-winter stream
Rippling up for spring and
The mountains a long way off
Telling us of beginnings.
Old Woman,
With you I knew
The peace of high places
And the meaning of a flower
Curled up against the wind
Or leaning toward the sun.
Old Woman,
In small things always
There was you as if
All nature contained your thoughts and so
I learned from rocks and rainbows
Tall trees and butterflies.

Old Woman,
There was you in the eagle
Flying free and lonely
And in the eyes of a deer
I saw once in an untamed place.
Old Woman,
There is you in all good things
That awaken me and say
My life was richer, fuller
Because you lived with me.

Hold on to what is good
even if it is
a handful of earth.
Hold on to what you believe
even if it is
a tree which stands by itself.
Hold on to what you must do
even if it is
a long way from here.
Hold on to life even when
it is easier letting go.
Hold on to my hand even when
I have gone away from you.

About the Author

NANCY WOOD grew up in New Jersey and "escaped West" when she was 22 years old. Despite her eastern beginnings, she has long been fascinated by our western and Indian heritages—a love which has produced *Little Wrangler*, a children's book; also *Colorado: Big Mountain Country*, a vivid portrait of the state and its people; a novel, *The Last Five-Dollar Baby;* and *Hollering Sun*, a poetic presentation of the beliefs, roots, and statements which best describe the uniqueness of Taos Pueblo. Most recently she has coauthored, with Roy Emerson Stryker, *In This Proud Land*, a photographic look at America, 1935–43. Ms. Wood now makes her home in Colorado Springs, Colorado.

About the Artist

FRANK HOWELL has coached wrestling, driven in auto races, and taught art to inner-city children, and he brings to his paintings and sculptures equal versatility in boldness and sensitivity.

Deeply interested in portraying contemporary Indian life, he lives in Breckenridge, Colorado, where he opened his own gallery in 1970, and he maintains a second studio in Taos, New Mexico.